READ

READ

READ

MW01093422

PARTS OF A FLOWER

PETAL

SEEDS

STEM

LEAF

ROOTS

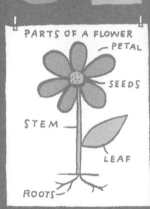

RED

ORANGE

YELLOW

GREEN

BLUE

PURPLE

WHITE

BROWN

1 2 3 4 5

PHOEBE
SOUNDS IT OUT

TO MARTHA, APRIL, SARAH, LIZ,
AND TEACHERS OF PHOEBES EVERYWHERE — J.Z.
TO MA AND PA — D.H.

Owlkids Books acknowledges the financial support of the Canada Council for the Arts,
the Ontario Arts Council, the Government of Canada through the Canada Book Fund
(CBF) and the Government of Ontario through the Ontario Media Development
Corporation's Book Initiative for our publishing activities.

Published in Canada by
Owlkids Books Inc.
10 Lower Spadina Avenue
Toronto, ON M5V 2Z2

Published in the United States by
Owlkids Books Inc.
1700 Fourth Street
Berkeley, CA 94710

Library and Archives Canada Cataloguing in Publication

Zwillich, Julie, author

        Phoebe sounds it out / written by Julie Zwillich ; illustrated by
Denise Holmes.

ISBN 978-1-77147-164-0 (hardback)

        I. Holmes, Denise, illustrator II. Title.

PZ7.1.Z85Ph 2017   j813'.6   C2016-905681-3

Library of Congress Control Number: 2016952837

The artwork in this book was rendered in ink and colored in Adobe Illustrator.
Edited by: Karen Li and Debbie Rogosin
Designed by: Claudia Dávila

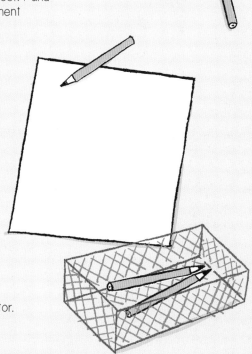

ONTARIO ARTS COUNCIL
CONSEIL DES ARTS DE L'ONTARIO
an Ontario government agency
un organisme du gouvernement de l'Ontario

Canada Council
for the Arts

Conseil des Arts
du Canada

Canadä

Manufactured in Dongguan, China, in December 2016, by Toppan Leefung Packaging &
Printing (Dongguan) Co, Ltd
Job #BAYDC31

A   B   C   D   E   F

Publisher of Chirp, chickaDEE and OWL
www.owlkidsbooks.com

Owlkids Books is a division of  Bayard
CANADA

PHOEBE SOUNDS IT OUT

written by
Julie Zwillich

illustrated by
Denise Holmes

Owlkids Books

Phoebe pulled on her rain boots. Mama called them galoshes and Grammy called them wellies, but Phoebe called them rain boots, because that was what they were for: splashing about in the rain. Phoebe liked her boots. A lot.

But it wasn't raining today. So Phoebe decided to call them sun boots. And now she was ready for school.

Phoebe's favorite teacher was Ms. Martha. She was kind and smart. When Ms. Martha saw Phoebe in her sun boots, she said, "Well, we'll just have to put the sprinklers on after lunch and splash around." Ms. Martha totally understood boots.

"But first," said Ms. Martha, "let's work on writing our names."

The other teacher, Ms. April, put a big basket of pencils on the table and got out her guitar. Ms. April liked singing better than talking.

Phoebe chose a pencil, and then decided putting her right sun boot on her left foot and her left sun boot on her right foot was more important.

Phoebe's toes felt wrong in her boots.

Ms. April sat down beside her. "Phoebe, we're writing our names. Give it a try."

Phoebe had seen her name before. Mama had even stitched it on her ladybug backpack. But it started with a *P* and had a whole lot of other letters that didn't make sense.

Phoebe figured her mother had made a mistake. She didn't want Mama to feel bad about it, because everyone makes mistakes, even mamas.

Phoebe put down her pencil and picked up another one. Then she held it under her nose and pretended it was a moustache. Ms. April was floating around the table singing quietly, "Just sound it out."

Phoebe sounded out the first letter of her name. "Fffff." This was certainly not how her name began on her backpack. *P* was for *popcorn* and *pencils*. She knew the letter that made the right sound: one line and two sticks.

The next sound was "Eeee." Phoebe drew one and threw in an extra so the first *e* wouldn't feel lonely.

Maybe that's what Mama was thinking
when she stitched that crazy *o*.

And now Phoebe was at a letter she loved. The only one that made sense on the ladybug backpack *and* when she sounded it out. A bubble and a stick. The hard part was getting it to face the right way.

At the end of her name was the "Eeee" sound again. Phoebe wanted to try something different. Maybe she could borrow the letter that was at the end of Nicky's name.

It sounded right. Nicky wouldn't mind.

Ms. Martha came over and looked at the children's work. "Something's not right," she said. She turned and walked away.

Phoebe's boots felt hot on her feet. Maybe
they really *were* only for rainy days.

Ms. Martha returned and placed a box on the table.
"We forgot to decorate our names with glitter glue!"

Phoebe liked glitter glue. A lot. She opened
the orange tube and squished it all over her
name. It sparkled and shone.

When Phoebe ran out of glitter glue, she switched her right sun boot onto her right foot and her left sun boot onto her left foot. *Ahhh*. That felt better.

Phoebe handed her name to Ms. Martha,
who smiled and said, "What a great start."